Keeper of the Stars

Keeper of the Stars

Written by Carol Lovelace

Illustrated by S.M.R. Cooper

Xulon Press
2301 Lucien Way #415
Maitland, FL 32751
407.339.4217
www.xulonpress.com

Printed in the United States of America.

Paperback ISBN-13: 978-1-66281-171-5
Ebook ISBN-13: 978-1-66281-172-2

A special thanks to Philip Black, you are a jewel in His crown.
In memory of Bob and Peggy, heaven couldn't wait.

High in the peaks of Wyoming was a
hidden lake called **Rainbow Lake.**
It was Olivia and Hayden's favorite place.

They played joyfully and happily in
God's loving grace.
He created the forest, a most
delightful and magical space.

7

Hummingbirds zoomed here and there
and scattered **butterflies everywhere.**

A **giant blue jay** with his
crazy black hair,
squawked and squeaked
at a **baby brown bear.**

8

They built a castle tall **and grand.**
They were now king and queen **of their own forest land.**

They gathered **pinecones, flowers, and stuff**, and made crowns that were certainly **grand enough.**

They fished and waded in the sparkling lake,
then flew a kite for the breeze to take.
A big, shy moose with a noble beard
wandered past them and they quietly cheered.

The forest grew dim, **the shadows grew long,**
and nature's music hushed
with the **cricket's soft song.**

Hayden and Olivia
snuggled deep in their flannels
and gazed at the Milky Way's bright,
starry channels.

They said their prayers, thanking God for His love.

He loved them before He threw the stars above.

He loved them before He made the dragonflies and bees.

He loved them before He created many things.

He loved them before He breathed the night sky.

He loved them before He painted dawn's pearl light.

He loved them before time began.

He loved them before He kept the stars in His hands.

CPSIA information can be obtained
at www.ICGtesting.com
Printed in the USA
LVRC101616170521
687666LV00003B/42

9781662811715